Dear Judah,

Judy Gibson is a friend of ours (and also of your family). She and I are in the Scribblers writing group. She mentioned us in The Acknowledgments on the back page. The Scribblers have signed; also Ken (the photographer) and Ken (our group leader).

Hope you enjoy.

We love you,

Charlene
&
Jimmy

Adventures

of

MISS PATTY'S GOOSE

and Other Friends

ISBN: 978-0-692-18817-0

Any references to historical events, real people, or real places are used fictitiously. Names, characters, and places are products of the author's imagination.

Front cover image by Ken Christison.
Book design by Vanessa A. Council.
Illustrations by Dianne Evans.

Printed by BookBaby, Inc., in the United States of America.

First printing edition 2018.

7905 N. Crescent Blvd.
Pennsauken, NJ 08110

www.bookbaby.com

Dedication

To the Young through the Elderly who have watched MISS PATTY'S GOOSE change from month to month, season to season and various events through the years, this book is lovingly dedicated.

Without your interest , comments and encouragement, the true life stories within the pages would be known to mostly a small rural community.

May each reader find enjoyment on every page.

iss Patty loved birds, but she was especially fond of geese.

Even when she was a little girl, she loved to watch geese flying in a V shape, making honking noises as they traveled. She decided this was their way of talking to each other. Honk! Honk! Honk!

One day when Miss Patty and Mr. Ben were on vacation, they stopped in a shop that had all kinds of things to sell. She looked around at cement frogs and squirrels climbing on tree limbs and kittens playing.

All of a sudden, Miss Patty saw a big white cement goose sitting in a corner. She was so excited she grabbed Mr. Ben's arm and almost dragged him over to the goose. When he saw the twinkle in her eyes, he bought the goose and brought it home with them.

Mr. Ben placed the goose in their yard where Miss Patty could see it from her kitchen window. She was happy she had her own goose, and, even though it was made of cement, she felt a warm connection to it.

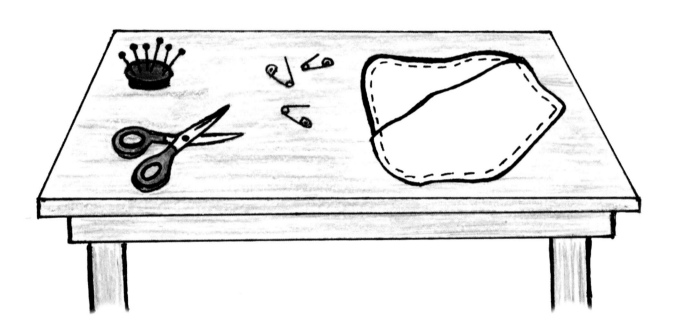

She wanted to make it a special goose and she decided to make clothes for it. "How do you make clothes for a goose?" she thought. She made a pattern, pinned it together, and placed it on the goose. It worked!

Then Miss Patty went shopping for material. She bought all colors and designs and started making clothes for her goose.

She decided to make an outfit for each holiday or season. When the stack of clothes was finished, Miss Patty started dressing her goose.

For January, she placed a warm coat with a fur collar on the goose. She made a top hat and placed fur around it. She imagined if there was a New Year's Eve Party, her goose would be ready to go! Then she placed a sign beside this gaily dressed goose, wishing all passers-by a Happy New Year!

February found the goose with the biggest red heart on its chest and a red top hat, making him look almost like "Cat in the Hat!" What a nice Valentine wish for everybody who may look his way. Neighbors were beginning to notice this unusual bird!

arch is always a windy month, and Miss Patty worried about the outfit for her goose.

Ah, Saint Patrick's Day is mid-month, so she scrambled among her green material and found the perfect green for a shamrock coat and another top hat with a huge silver buckle aglow on the front of the hat. She secured it tightly on the goose's head so the wind could not blow it off.

pril is the month of rain showers and spring flowers. Miss Patty fashioned the neatest yellow raincoat and hat for her goose.

Easter comes in April almost every year. So she made a beautiful spring dress with flowers of pink and lavender and a fancy hat to match. She then placed a white cross beside the goose to rejoice in the resurrection of Jesus Christ!

When the month of May arrives, all Spring flowers are in full bloom, migrating birds have returned to Miss Patty's yard and the days are warm and sunny. The important event of this month is Mothers Day! She dressed the goose in a pretty, frilly dress, a hat, and set a pot of flowers at her feet. This was to remind everyone to remember to let their moms know how much she is loved and appreciated.

June is a very happy time for young people because they graduate from school; some from kindergarten, some from elementary, and some from high school. Even with a college only a few miles away, Miss Patty knew those students also proudly marched to graduation music. Mr. Goose was dressed in his graduation gown, his mortarboard hat and diploma. He wore a gold tassel on his hat which is worn by an honor student.

Also, brides like to get married in June, so later in the month of June, the Goose became a bride.

July is such a hot month that the goose wore three outfits: 1) July 4th is an important national holiday for the United States of America. It is called Independence Day because the Declaration of Independence was signed in 1776, making us a free nation. We are so proud of our nation that we fly the national flag in many places all year, but on July 4th, there are flags flying everywhere. U.S. stands for the United States, but through the years, we adopted the name "Uncle Sam" dressed in red and white striped trousers, a blue coat and wearing a striped top hat as a symbol for our nation. Miss Patty made an "Uncle Sam" outfit for her goose, and now he was all ready for the July 4th holiday. 2) Many vacations are taken this month, especially to the beach where sand sticks to feet and the sun gets extremely hot.

s a reminder of the cooling effect of a brisk swim, Miss Patty fashioned a bathing suit and a floppy hat to screen the goose's beak.
3) Everybody looks forward to the juicy taste of a sweet watermelon during this hot month.

In Miss Patty's town, there is a Watermelon Festival, which is the last few days of July, and Miss Patty smiled as she made a big green watermelon with a stem hat for her beloved goose to complete the July wardrobe.

ugust, with sunflowers blooming and bees buzzing, found the goose dressed as a sunflower the first part of the month and a bumble bee the last weeks. These outfits were given to Miss Patty for her goose.

September found the goose in his school clothes with a lunchbox hanging from his shoulder. Each morning he watched as the school bus came by. Smiling children were looking out a window of the bus, pointing at this interesting old goose.

Late in the month, Miss Patty put a football uniform on her goose and placed a football under his wing. Now he was ready to kick off the football season!

October! How could Miss Patty dress her goose for this colorful month? It was harvest time, so she bought him a little red wagon, and she filled it with a pumpkin, ears of corn and beautiful fall leaves. She made a pair of overalls, a colorful shirt and a slouch hat, making the Goose ready to help harvest crops. Then, as Halloween drew near, the Goose became a witch with a long black dress and a very tall, pointed hat. Miss Patty placed a big smiling pumpkin beside the Goose, and neighboring children enjoyed passing by and waving.

November, the month of Thanksgiving and hunting for a turkey. The Goose was seen wearing a hunting suit, a small gun slung over his shoulder and a little Beagle dog stood proudly beside him. He was ready for the big hunt! This outfit lasted until late November.

Miss Patty was beginning to think of Thanksgiving and why this holiday was celebrated. She thought of how the Indians taught the first settlers many good ways about raising crops and they also introduced the early settlers to new foods. She thought it proper to dress the Goose as Pocahontas, a lovely Indian maid. She also thought she might dress the goose as a turkey, but she knew there was not a goose anywhere that wanted to be a turkey. The very idea!

December brings many things to mind, and Miss Patty had a hard time deciding how to dress her Goose. Santa Claus is popular all month, so she made a red and white suit with a matching hat. She found a sleigh and placed the Goose in it and she packed toys and gifts around him. There were no reindeer. But wait! She could use two large plastic geese she had packed away in the barn. She asked Mr. Ben to fashion deer horns to place atop their heads; she made reins of shining ribbons and was pleased with her Goose.

Christmas is a time to celebrate the birthday of Jesus Christ. Miss Patty put candles in her windows and a big star at the top of her Christmas tree. Several angels circled the star, showing that a star shone over the baby Jesus, and angels sang about His birth. There were many gifts under her tree, but she knew the greatest gift ever given was Jesus, our Savior.

As the year ended, Miss Patty recalled the many good remarks friends, neighbors and strangers had said about her Goose. One particular lady had been very sick for a long time and made many trips by Miss Patty's house as she visited doctors. "This goose is very special; he makes me smile and feel much better. I'm sure both children and grownups enjoy seeing this colorful figure. Please continue dressing him," she said.

Of course, this made Miss Patty happy and she was so glad Mr. Ben had purchased the Goose years ago.

Female Junco
© Ken Christison 2008

Miss Patty's other Friends.

kenskritters

American Goldfinch

Miss Patty had other friends, and they were real birds. She and Mr. Ben welcomed all kinds of birds to their yard. They had bird feeders filled with seeds, nuts and dried fruits; they had two bird baths which allowed the birds to have fresh cool water and also to take quick baths. It was a joy to watch them bathing. They would fly into the water, flap their wings, which sent sprays of water in all directions, then duck their heads underwater while furiously shaking their feathers. However, sometimes there was trouble at the bird baths – fights began when one or more birds wanted their time to play, while a little greedy bird stayed too long. Eventually, they learned to share.

kenskritters

Northern Cardinal

The most colorful birds that visited were a pair of cardinals. The male cardinal was the most beautiful bright red with a fluff or crest of feathers on top of his head and a black face. The female had a brown body with dull red feathers on her wings, tail and fluff on her head. Occasionally, Miss Patty heard them singing in happy little chirps.

kenskritters

Sparrow

There were more sparrows at Miss Patty's feeders and the birdbaths than other birds. All seemed to have brown, black, olive or gray feathers, mostly mingled together with streaks on their bodies and wings. They were quite small birds, with many different songs. Miss Patty noticed some had pretty tunes, and some songs were dull off-key.

kenskritters

Eastern Bluebird

One of Miss Patty's favorites was the Eastern Bluebird. His upper body and wings were bright blue, while underneath was rusty orange with a white belly. His voice was a soft little song that Miss Patty was soon able to recognize. Mr. Ben had two bird boxes that he had carefully made and mounted on poles for bluebirds. He knew Bluebirds wanted the opening to their house to face the east, which would warm baby birds early in the mornings after a cool night. They also enjoyed their houses not too close where other birds lived. If they liked their house and its location, they would return each Spring to the same house to raise their babies.

Blue Jay

The Blue Jay was a handsome bird, but not a favorite. He had blue and white feathers on his upper body and wings and he had a white belly. He had a blue topknot with a few black feathers on his head and face. He chased smaller birds away and had a shrill voice. However, smaller birds regarded him as necessary because he warned them when danger was near, like hawks and owls, who like to eat small birds. Whenever he started screeching and flying from tree to tree, Miss Patty or Mr. Ben would run outside and make loud noises to chase away the bad birds and protect their birds from dangerous predators.

kenskritters

American Robin

After a long, cold winter, Mr. Ben eagerly awaited to hear Miss Patty's excited voice calling him. "Ben, come quick! The Robins are back and that means Spring is here." Sure enough, near the feeder was a big, stately bird with a dark grayish-brown back and wing feathers with brilliant orange underneath. He would eat his fill of nuts and seeds, then he would run across the yard and sing a cheery song, which Miss Patty believed was "I'm so glad to be back!"

Hummingbird

Not often did Mr. Ben interfere with Miss Patty and her birds, but his favorite birds were the hummingbirds, and their return was another sure sign that Spring had come. If Miss Patty had not hung hummingbird feeders by April 1, Mr. Ben would surely remind her. It was a certainty that between April 1 and April 4, the "hummers" would be back! One year when they returned early, no feeders were up and Miss Patty was startled to see a Red-throated Hummingbird at her kitchen window, little wings whirling, his voice muttering twittering squeaks and his tiny eyes snapping. Instantly, Miss Patty ran around, got the feeders ready with syrupy nectar, and Mr. Ben quickly hung the first one at the kitchen window for his hungry little friend's first feast of Spring. They were a delight to watch all summer, but by mid-September, they were gone. Instead of being sad, Miss Patty and Mr. Ben knew they would return with the coming Spring.

Red-Headed Woodpecker

For several days, Miss Patty had heard a rat-tat-tat outside, but she could not figure where or what the sound was. Finally, she called Mr. Ben to track down what was going on. He found a red-headed woodpecker pecking on a big pecan tree in their yard. Then he would fly to the housetop and pitch on the chimney to continue pecking. This was quite rare for a woodpecker to be seen near the house. He continued coming each day and Miss Patty noticed he started chasing other birds away from the feeders and birdbaths. She watched him and decided he was unwelcomed in her yard. She would clap her hands and angrily shout for him to leave. He would fly up to the chimney on the rooftop, his red head shining and his brilliant white feathers gleaming in the sun.

Red-Headed Woodpecker

One day Mr. Ben called and asked Miss Patty to come quickly. He said, "Willie Woodpecker has fallen down the chimney!"

The old couple didn't know what to do! Finally, Mr. Ben went inside the house, opened a hole covering the bottom of the chimney and out flew Willie Woodpecker! He was covered in black soot and looked like a crow (which is a large solid black bird). Miss Patty caught him in her apron and wiped off as much soot as she could. Mr. Ben checked Willie and decided he was not hurt, and so they opened the back door, and away he flew and they did not see him for several days.

Red-Headed Woodpecker

When he returned, he looked pitiful. His beautiful white chest was gray, his brilliant red head was not shiny any more, and he timidly flew to the feeder and ate with other birds; then he flew to the bath and took a long, splashy bath. Miss Patty noticed he did not try to run other birds away.

Many baths later, he returned to his beautiful self, but he had learned he was no longer "king of Miss Patty's yard:" he was just one of her friends. He had learned a very humble lesson.

Rooster

As Miss Patty thought of her bird friends, she remembered years before when her young son was doing his daily run for track competition and he found a small, baby chick beside the country road where he was running. He stopped, looked at him closely and saw he was ok and hoped someone would come along and find him. As he continued his run, so did this ball of white fluff. The faster he ran, so did the baby chicken! He stuffed the little creature in his shirt, and, when he came home, he convinced his Mom there was nothing to do but bring this little creature home.

Rooster

Miss Patty fed it bread crumbs and small hamburger bites, and the little critter thrived! Mr. Ben got a large box and put it on the porch for this "temporary visitor's home." It started getting feathers to replace the down, but it was not known if this would be a rooster or hen. Mr. Ben said it was a hen and Miss Patty said it would be a rooster.

They decided to name it Mo and, if it was a rooster, he would be Elmo, and if a hen, she would be Molly. However, as a term of endearment, it was called Mosey. Weeks passed and the mystery was not solved, but now, there was a big chicken living in a box on the porch. One morning as Miss Patty fixed breakfast, she heard a weird noise on the porch – almost like a strangling. She ran to make sure the chicken was all right. No more sounds.

Rooster

The next morning there was that sound, but different, more like a cock-a-doddle-do. She ran into the bedroom, shook Mr. Ben and said, "We have us a rooster. I was right!"

Elmo, known as Mosey, grew into a huge white rooster and was beautiful. However, he had no chicken friends and began to wander away from the yard. A friend who lived on a farm with many chickens offered to take him, and when Mr. Ben & Miss Patty carried him to the farm, he was welcomed into the flock and all ended well with Mosey.

Pigeon

Mr. Ben worked in a big building with a very high ceiling. Pigeons would build nests high up in the ceiling and lay eggs. In a short while, baby pigeons would hatch, and the process of being fed worms began. Soon their little pink bodies were covered with yellow fuzz and they would become active and start moving around in the nest. Sad to say, sometimes, one would fall out of the nest to the floor below and most times it died.

Mr. Ben had eaten his lunch and was getting ready to return to work. Plomp! A little yellow fuzzy thing lay close to his foot. And yes, it was a baby pigeon.
Mr. Ben picked him up, opened his lunchbox, wrapped this tiny thing in a napkin and set him aside. When he got off work, he picked up his lunchbox and rushed home to Miss Patty. "Patty, I have brought you a gift and you must open it immediately," Mr. Ben said.

Pigeon

She quickly opened the lunchbox and there lay the tiny baby pigeon. He was hungry, he was cold and he needed his mother to snuggle up to. Miss Patty instantly became his mother! She fed him tiny bread crumbs, pieces of a worm Mr. Ben had found in the yard and gave him water from a medicine dropper. When he was fed, she dropped him in her apron pocket where he snuggled down and went to sleep. Thus began his life as "a little person" and was named Leroy.

Leroy had a little nest in the corner of a cage, and as he grew, he would come out of the cage and follow Miss Patty and Mr. Ben around the house. Soon he could flap his tiny wings, making them strong for flying. Miss Patty kept a jar of popcorn on the cabinet, and his first flight was from the floor to the cabinet and his jar of popcorn!

Pigeon

Mr. Ben said Leroy was ready to live outside and begin his life as a bird. He took Leroy to a nearby field, patted his head and wished him well. Miss Patty was on the porch with tears in her eyes. Leroy did not know what to do, so he just sat in Mr. Ben's hands and looked around. Mr. Ben threw him up in the air and shouted, "Fly Leroy, fly away!" And he did!

That is not the end of the story. When Mr. Ben got back to the porch, Leroy had gotten there first and he was making a happy pigeon sound, sitting on Miss Patty's shoulder, and Miss Patty was shaking with laughter. He did live outside, but came in each day to fill up on popcorn out of his jar on the cabinet. When guests came to the house, Leroy would land on the roof of their car, strut around in a circle, uttering his pigeon noise and welcome them.

Pigeon

For several years, he brought much joy to Miss Patty, Mr. Ben and many friends. It is believed he finally decided it was time to start a family of his own and went in search of a wife.

Miss Patty and Mr. Ben enjoyed many birds through the years. They always provided them with food, water and love. But Miss Patty's favorite bird was the old white cement goose that she shared with neighbors and friends.

Acknowledgments

My sincere gratitude to those instrumental in the production
of this book:

Dianne Evans, who humored my imagination about the book's
possibility, and brought "the Goose" to life with her creative artwork;
Ken Christison, the most talented, yet humble photographer, with
a phenomenal photography reputation; and Vanessa A. Council, the
"master weaver" who took facts, ideas, pictures and with her computer
skills and actual "know how" wove our efforts into reality; to Ken
Wolfskill and the Scribblers for advice and encouragement; and finally,
to young and old family, friends and unknowns who have admired Miss
Patty's Goose over the years.

Thank You!